THE YEAR WE LEARNED TO FLY

JACQUELINE WOODSON

illustrated by RAFAEL LÓPEZ

 NANCY PAULSEN BOOKS

For Kaze. —J.W.

To Esteban Hotesse and the Tuskegee Airmen. —R.L.

NANCY PAULSEN BOOKS

An imprint of Penguin Random House LLC, New York

Nancy Paulsen Books and colophon are trademarks of Penguin Random House LLC.

Visit us online at penguinrandomhouse.com

Library of Congress Cataloging-in-Publication Data
Names: Woodson, Jacqueline, author. | López, Rafael, 1961– illustrator.
Title: The year we learned to fly / Jacqueline Woodson; illustrated by Rafael López.
Description: New York: Nancy Paulsen Books, [2022] | Summary: "By heeding their wise grandmother's advice, a brother and sister discover
the ability to lift themselves up and imagine a better world"—Provided by publisher.
Identifiers: LCCN 2021017763 | ISBN 9780399545535 (hardcover) | ISBN 9780399545542 (ebook) | ISBN 9780399545566 (ebook)
Subjects: CYAC: Imagination—Fiction. | Brothers and sisters—Fiction. | Grandmothers—Fiction. | African Americans—Fiction. | LCGFT: Picture books.
Classification: LCC PZ7.W868 Ye 2022 | DDC [E]—dc23
LC record available at https://lccn.loc.gov/2021017763

Manufactured in the USA
ISBN 9780399545535
1 3 5 7 9 10 8 6 4 2

PC

Design by Marikka Tamura
Text set in Siseriff LT Std
The illustrations were created with a combination of acrylic paint on wood,
pen and ink, pencil, and watercolors, and put together digitally in Photoshop.

*T*hat was the year we learned to fly . . .

That was the spring when the rain seemed like it
would never stop
and the thunder boomed so hard,
we weren't allowed to go outside.

Use those beautiful and brilliant minds of yours,
my grandmother said.

Lift your arms,
close your eyes,
take a deep breath,
and believe in a thing.
Somebody somewhere at some point
was just as bored as you are now.

So my brother and I closed our eyes.
And for a few minutes that first day,
we weren't stuck in our apartment anymore.

We were flying over the city we'd known
our whole lives, but
it was suddenly different. Exploding
with every kind of flower
we'd ever dreamed of growing.

That was the summer we learned to fly,
when my brother and I couldn't stop fussing with each other
over whose turn it was to wash the windows,
to feed the dog, to clean the kitchen.

We fought and frowned and made silent promises
to never speak to each other ever again.

My grandmother said,

Lift your arms,
close your eyes,
take a deep breath,
and stop being so mean about everything.
Somebody somewhere at some point
was just as mad as you are now.

So we did. And as the soft wind
took us out over the city and past the windows
of kids who hadn't yet learned to fly, my brother and I reached for
each other's hand, flying and diving and laughing,
and leaving all of our mad far behind us.

That was the autumn our rooms felt too big and lonely
with only us in them and the darkness coming on so fast.
But while we hugged ourselves against the too-quiet of it all,
we remembered
that we didn't have to be stuck anywhere anymore.

My grandmother had learned to fly
from the people who came before.

They were aunts and uncles and cousins
who were brought here on huge ships,
their wrists and ankles cuffed in iron,
but, my grandmother said,
nobody can ever cuff
your beautiful and brilliant mind.

So our people learned to fly, she said.
They dreamed a thing and made it happen.
Closed their eyes and flew away home.

Lift your arms, my grandmother said, *close your eyes,*
and remember somebody somewhere at some point
had to figure out they could fly.

That was the winter we moved away
from the building and the block and the friends
we'd always known

to a street where the kids looked at us funny
and didn't even answer when we asked them
if they wanted to play.
It's okay, I said to my brother.
*Somebody somewhere at some point
had to figure out they were ready
for any new thing coming their way.*

So like the people who came before us, we lifted our arms
even higher, closed our eyes even tighter, breathed in even deeper,
and flew the way we'd always known how to—
free as the aunties and uncles and cousins
who'd come before us,
free as our own beautiful and brilliant minds.

For a long time, the kids on the ground watched us . . .

then one by one
they lifted their arms.
One by one
they too
learned to fly.

The first time I read *The People Could Fly: American Black Folktales* by the brilliant Virginia Hamilton, I realized that through her beautiful story, I was learning to fly. Not with wings, but with words. Her book is the story of how enslaved people escaped their hard lives by lifting up and flying away home, and every page is anointed with the illustrious paintings of Leo and Dianne Dillon.

As a kid, I always wondered how people were able to survive through the horrors of enslavement. But they did. And they passed down their stories and their fables and their memories to the young people coming along after them. And these stories gave us wings.

Virginia Hamilton gave me and so many other writers storytelling wings. And with these wings, I have been able to "fly" past even the hardest of times into the world of my stories.

Sometimes the first step toward change is closing our eyes, taking a breath, and imagining a different way.

—Jacqueline Woodson